TEACHER TEACHER

Darrell N. Etienne Jr.

authorHOUSE®

AuthorHouse™
1663 Liberty Drive
Bloomington, IN 47403
www.authorhouse.com
Phone: 1 (800) 839-8640

Published by AuthorHouse 07/12/2018

ISBN: 978-1-5462-4845-3 (sc)
ISBN: 978-1-5462-4844-6 (e)

Library of Congress Control Number: 2018907453

Print information available on the last page.

CONTENTS

DEDICATION

This book is dedicated to my mom

the greatest teacher I know.

YOUR TYPICAL BOY

Yup, I wear them KD's, Foamposets, Jordans, Lebrons and even Hurraches. South Park is my favorite show to watch, which my mom very much hates.

"It's inappropriate," she'd say. "It has way too much profanity," she continued to rant.

After it kept showing up on my television set, she resolved to simply inform me that she didn't expect to hear any of those words coming out of my mouth.

My phone and I have a great relationship. Snapchat, streaks, Instagram, House Party, and yes You Tube, are all a part of what I do on my smart phone. Friends are made and lost because of streaks. Streaks on Snapchat are how many consecutive days that you send pictures back and forth. You can't miss a day. When people would lose our streaks, yes I would unfriend them. Nope, I would never start up a new streak with that particular person ever again. It is that serious. House Party is another app that I use. Up to eight people can be on face time at once.

I play NBA2K, FIFA, and GTA (which my mom also says is inappropriate). I connect with friends and others on Xbox live. The headset keeps all of our conversation discrete. I find time for this mostly on the weekends. My weekday evenings are usually spent at soccer practice or doing homework. Some nights are less hectic than others.

My spare time is also spent playing basketball, or jumping on the trampoline, or yes playing more soccer. My music is sometimes playing in the background during these actives or not. I love hip-hop music. There ain't nothing like Hip Hop music (Groove B. Chill). It gets me hyped, helps me relax, and plays when my alarm goes off in the morning. Some of my favorites are rappers like 2 Chains, Drake, J. Cole, Kendrick Lamar, Travis Scott, Dave East, and Kodak Black.

I also like old school rappers. You can thank my parents for this. I love the stories these rappers tell and the depth of their lyrics. Rakim, Tribe Called Quest, Onyx, Lost Boyz, Jay Z are a few of my favorites. I can't forget Tupac and Biggie. Yes I like them both controversial or not.

My playlist is impressively long. Some of the featured songs are Throw Ya Gunz by Onyx, Good Drank by 2 Chains, Who Shot Ya by Biggie, So Ghetto by Jay Z, Rymes Galore by Busta Rhymes, and Hit'em Up by 2Pac. As I said, the list does go on but I am going to stop there.

RIDICULOUSNESS

WELL THE SUMMER IS over and I'm off to 5th Grade. I was warned about what to expect from this school and its teachers. Most of which I saw firsthand because I was in a neighboring school for three and a half years.

I couldn't even grab my disgusting lunch and sit down peacefully before the entertainment began. Two fights erupted simultaneously. Both fights were on opposite sides of the cafeteria. My head was moving back and forth between the fights just like a game of Ping-Pong. On the left side of the court, a girl was pulling out another girl's hair. On the right side of the court, one guy slammed the other guy on the lunch table. On the left side, the girl who got her hair pulled out grabs the other girl by her shirt and rips it. On the right side, lunch trays and food are flying around. People jumped up, backed away and ducked down so food wouldn't get on their nice outfits. Remember, it was the first day of school, and usually everyone has on their best gear.

This may sound crazy but people were enjoying it, self-included! Some of the spectators were laughing and others were recording as they yelled, "World Star". When people have their phones out, recording, and saying, "World Star," they are getting ready to post the fight on World Star, the fight-posting website. *HMMM! You're a World Star because you're fighting? OKAY! This was the epitome of ridiculousness.*

On the left side, Ms. Gabriel flies into the cafeteria like superwoman to break up the fight between the girls. On the right side, Dr. Hulk barrels in angrily and breaks up the fight between the two boys. "IT'S THE FIRST DAY OF SCHOOL!!! WHY Y'ALL FIGHT'N ALREADY?" Dr. Hulk loudly questioned, with a puzzled look on his face. No one answered. After the question, Ms. Gabriel stormed out with the four people who fought, and marched them right into her office, the Principal's office. Things didn't look very good for them at all. As a matter of fact, based on how things went down on my first day of school this was going to be a very different school year.

{ 3 }

MS. HOT BREATH

SAME DAY PERIOD 5 I met Ms. Hot Breath. As soon as we all settled down into our assigned seats, she began to yell at the kids. She would get up in kids' faces. Her breath was hot and it reeked of coffee and cigarettes. *UGGH! Why would you come up in someone's face that close if your breath is hot and smells like that?*

She would begin, "This is not how you are supposed to act on school grounds. If you act like that at home that's ok but don't do that here!!!" It didn't stop there.

"You all are just like my two ex-husbands, obnoxious and careless!" *Did she really just say this to us on the very first day of school?* None of us liked her. Most of the class absolutely hated her.

Every time she opened up her mouth, she would be yelling about something. Instead of teaching us English Language Arts, it would be yell at the kids.

"Shut the hell up! Mind your damn business! Yes, this is how she would talk to us. Actually, it wasn't talking at all, it was yelling. Yelling all of the time. I mean ALL OF THE TIME!!! On many days we barley even had time to learn. When Ms. Hot Breath was supposed to be teaching, she would be ranting. She would be ranting about her marriages, and then, the class period would over. Her actions were not what I expected from a teacher at all; especially from a white teacher that is teaching in the hood. My expectation was that she would be kind, respectful, and more self-conscious. I was expecting her to be self-conscious enough to brush her teeth really good in the morning and maybe even use some mouthwash. If you're going to be yelling in kids face you should certainly do this! So much of the opposite of what I expected with this teacher happened.

I was the victim of her hot breath yelling rants! YUCK! *UGGH!* I wanted to stand up and yell right back at her. *GET OUT OF MY FACE! You do know your breath stinks right? Stay out of my face and everyone else's!"* But I didn't because I know much better than this. She was the adult and I was the student, the black student at that.

Whenever she would yell at me, according to her, my response always sounded as if I had an attitude. I probably did have one. Her breath was enough to give anyone an attitude. However, I always responded politely, as I was taught to do. Nevertheless as polite as I tried to be there was ALWAYS a command followed by an accusation of some sort.

"Joshua you need to work faster," she would bark.

"O.K. Ms. Hot Breath," I would calmly answer back.

"Oh my Lord, how disgusting, you have such a bad attitude," she would bellow.

As much as I wanted to *say, "Hey lady, are we on the same planet? Are we having the same conversation? I responded to you calmly!"* All I said was O.K. and you have a problem with that? I didn't. I just stayed quiet and kept working.

One day a girl named Ja'Lisha came into class late with Dunkin Donuts. She had a bagel and an orange juice in her hand. Breakfast had long been over, so I and the rest of the class was wondering what she was doing.

Ms. Hot Breath began screaming, "Ja'Lisha why are you strolling in here late with food like you're an important, beautiful princess?"

Ja'Lisha yells back, "First, I'm late with food because I'm hungry. What the Fu** do you do to food when you are hungry? You eat it. Two, I am beautiful." Ja'Lisha flipped the left side of her hair back and walked to her seat. As the confrontation between the two of them continued I began to laugh like there was no tomorrow. I mean this was some funny stuff.

"Joshua, you're disgusting. You like when people are arguing?" Ms. Hot Breath said to me. How did I get into this? I wasn't the only one laughing. Of course I am the one she wants to call out though. SMH!

"No, I don't like when people are arguing. That was funny though," I responded.

"You have such a nasty attitude you know?" Ms. Hot Breath replied in anger.

This was getting old! It was a good thing that I know who I am. She never had anything positive to say to me. I was getting tired of her and tired of her comments. This time I had a little more to say.

"Ms. Hot Breath I don't have an attitude. I'm talking to you in my regular voice. I use this same voice at home with my parents and they don't think or say that I have an attitude when I speak using the same tone."

"Joshua go to Ms. Gabriel's office!" she yelled. *Unbelievable I'm going to the principal's office for what exactly? You're mad because I am standing up for myself? You're really mad because Ja'Lisha called you on your comments to her. You're mad because you know you want to put her in her place but you are afraid to. You'd rather target me. Whatever!*

I got up and walked out of the class. *Little did Ms. HB know, I never minded going to Ms. Gabriel's office. We got along just fine. This wasn't a punishment at all. It was actually a nice change of scenery. We weren't learning a thing in class anyway.*

Ms. Gabriel greeted me, "Hello Joshua, what seems to be the problem with Ms. Hot Breath this time?"

While sighing and shaking my head I blurt, "All year long she's been saying that I have an attitude. I let it go time after time after time again. I said nothing every single time I heard her false statement, until today. I responded to her statement, she didn't like it, and so she sent me to your office. By the way this office is quite nice!"

"Thank – you", Mrs. Gabriel replied. "Your mother is Akilaz correct?"

"Yes," I nodded and said.

"I know your mom," she continued, "I also know that she has taught you better than to do what Ms. HB is saying you are doing in the class."

"So what are you saying?" I questioned in slight fear.

"Well what I am saying is this; I don't exactly believe a word that comes out of Ms. Hot Breath's rather smelly mouth. Nevertheless, there will be a lot of people who really can't handle your assertive style of communication. I am sure your mom taught you this. People will handle it better when you guys are all older. It's not your time yet," she concluded.

I shook my head saying "Okay." I knew what she was saying was right.

"Now get back to class Mr. Stevens. No more visits from you today," she encouraged.

Back to class I went with my head up and a big smile on my face. That experience was not a punishment at all. It was a very much-needed break. As soon as I happily walked back into Ms. Hot Breath's class, you guessed it she killed my vibe.

"Why are you smiling?" she barked, "You just got yourself in trouble and sent to the principal's office.

I stood still staring at her for five seconds pondering how I would respond. I decided to turn the other cheek because this confrontation was NOT worth my energy.

I continued to walk to my seat and got right to my work. Days continued to go by with her seeming to look for a chance to get at me. Every time she did though I would SMH and keep doing whatever I was doing.

Today was Ms. Hot Breath's birthday. I absolutely love birthdays. Before school, I decided I wanted to get her a gift. I stopped at the corner store and bought her some chewy red and white-striped mints. Right before my class with her, I sneakily slipped the present on her desk with a note that read "HAPPY BIRTHDAY MS. HOT BREATH - JOSHUA". As unbelievable as this may seem, I really was not trying to be offensive. I wanted to do something nice and I wasn't spending a lot of money. Plus she needed mints.

She waited until the end of class to acknowledge my gift out loud and in front of everyone.

"So you think I have bad breath, HUH?" she blurted angrily.

The truth was YES I did. Everyone knew it. But, nope I didn't respond! I just walked away into my next class hoping that she would enjoy her birthday. I definitely wasn't going to get into any back and forth with her today.

Later that day I found out that some of my friends and associates, Syron, Zy'eema, Noivas, and Gianna found out about the gift I gave Ms. Hot Breath. Apparently, some of my classmates had spread the news about my gift. My good intentions were taken the wrong way. In fact, my gift was used to "roast" her. (She would yell at a kid, and they would be mad about it. Next thing you know, BAM, my gift was the shot.)

"That's why Joshua got you mints for your birthday, with your stink breath," they would say with contempt.

Believe it or not, I inspired people. When Christmas rolled around my classmates gave her similar gifts but they took it to the next level. They gave her tongue scrapers, toothbrushes, toothpastes and even a small travel sized Listerine mouthwash. *Merry Christmas Ms. Hot Breath, hope you enjoyed your gifts.*

I KNOW I CAN'T TEACH MATH

"I KNOW I CAN
BE WHAT I WANNA BE
IF I WORK HARD AT IT
I'LL BE WHERE I WANNA BE."
(NASIR JONES, 2002).

WE HAD TO SAY this in concert almost every single day before we entered math class. Although I may have liked the song and didn't mind repeating the rap I needed to learn math. Unfortunately, this very rarely happened. Let me explain. The first time we ever had to do this, Ms. Slims accompanied the rap with a loud announcement.

"When you get inside this hot classroom, DO THE WORK!"

My question was, "What work?" I actually thought it and didn't have to say it.

T'schelle calmly asked, "UMMMMM Ms. Slims, what work?"

"Go to the office right now," Ms. Slims growled.

T'shelle started crying, got up and ran to Ms. Gabriel's office. After this encounter, I had further confirmation that this was going to be a very long and problem filled year. Each new day proved that I was correct in my assessment.

Something else we would hear quite often is, "Don't forget to tell your parents to complain to 70 Dover so we could get some money and some supplies." Every day like clockwork the same thing, "Don't forget to tell your parents to complain to 70 Dover so we could get some money for air conditions and iPads".

Certain days of class were more brutal than others. When we walked in the room and there were place value problems on the board, I knew it would be one of those days. I understood the math (today) just fine but many of my classmates struggled. *UGGH!!!... She is not going to teach she is going to yell and scream and tell us to DO THE WORK. I never could figure out how they were going to DO THE WORK if they didn't know how.*

The period was almost over on this particularly brutal day. Before we were dismissed, Ms. Slims told us that for homework we needed to write a poem/rap as a group about place value. When my group members were announced, I was good. I would be working with my friends Zyron, Janvion, and Christian. I knew we would ace this assignment. I would ask for the help of my dad who is a phenomenal poet.

When I got home that evening, I couldn't wait to get started on the assignment. Yes, my dad was ready to help me with it. We came up with this cool rap for the group. Everyone had a part and it was going to be lit. It went something like this:

I WAKE UP EVERY MORNING AND I GO TO SCHOOL

SOMETIMES IT'S WEAK AND SOMETIMES IT'S COOL

I DON'T WANNA BE A FOOL SO I JUST LISTEN

LEARNED ABOUT THE PLACE VALUE WHICH IS THE DIGITS POSITION

TAKE A NUMBER AND SEE WHAT THE VALUE IZ

HANDLING MY BIZ

EVEN THOUGH I'M NOT A WIZ

WANNA FIND THE PLACE VALUE OF A # THIS IS WHERE YOU START

LOOK AT THE PLACE VALUE CHART

WHEN THE # IS 365

THE #IN THE ONES PLACE IS THE #5

NOW TAKE A GLANCE OVER 1 PLACE TO THE LEFT

THE # IS 6 AND THERE IS ONE MORE LEFT

THE # 3 IS IN THE HUNDREDS PLACE

PLACE VALUE IS FUN AND EASY

PLEASE BELIEVE ME

THE # IS 365 AND THAT'S NO LIE

HOPE WE TAUGHT YOU SOMETHING

NOW WERE GONNA SAY GOODBYE.

I printed copies of the rap for the group so we were ready. Thinking about their personalities I also wrote the names of who was saying what part, besides the verses. Everybody was all set to take it home to study.

When we met up the next morning, everyone was excited to tell me that they remembered their part. When we began to practice, I was happy because everyone went through their part smoothly. That was everyone except for Christian. He didn't remember his part fully and the parts that he did remember were muffled and slurred. This came as a shocker to the group. He never talked like that before and he didn't have a speech problem.

He finally got his life together and we told Ms. Slims that we were ready to present in front of the whole class. The rap started out okay, until we got to Chris. He was slow to say his part and turns out he didn't remember his part at all.

"W – W – W anna find out how to say the number," was exactly what he said and sounded like.

As he continued to talk in the slow manner Javion screamed, "N*gga, what are you doing?"

Ms. Slims laughed out loud and so did the rest of the class.

"I know you can't talk, rap, or flow, sit down now. I'm pulling you from the group and your grade for this project is not a big a*s zero!" Slims bellowed loudly.

The whole time I'm thinking, I know you can't teach math. You shouldn't have anything to say. I kept it to myself. Christian walked back to his seat surprisingly unbothered by the whole scene. Yes it was a scene, a big ridiculous scene.

"Sooooooo what do we do now?" Zyron asked Ms. Slims in great aggravation.

"Ya'll got 30 seconds to figure it out!" she blurts out agitatedly.

We immediately got into a huddle to begin discussions.

"What are we going to do? Whose gonna do Chris's part?" Zyron asked.

"You got ten more seconds," we hear in the background.

I say, "I will do Chris's part since I know the whole rap, cool?"

"Cool!" the other members of the group respond.

"We're ready!" Javion exclaims.

"Good because I would've failed you guys too if it took you longer than 30 seconds!" said Ms. Slims.

"Ignore her guys and stay focused!" I whispered to them.

Now that Chris was gone, the order went Javion, Zyron, me and then me again. We repeated this order twice through. Both my fists began beating on the desk sounding the dope beat I created for us. When we began, I must admit I was feeling a lot of doubt. I was worried my group members weren't going to rise to the occasion at all. But they did! We destroyed it! We did so well that even Ms. Slims was smiling and screaming.

"Okay, ya'll flow like Nas," she blurted out, "I guess ya'll get an "A".

We were feeling delighted! Who doesn't like an "A"? It was much deeper than an easy A for me. It felt great because she was always so mean and angry. I never saw her respond like that to anyone. She was not the type to rejoice like she was in church praising God, over a child's project. She was always grumpy. But we did it! We made someone like her smile, feel good, and compliment students. A major accomplishment indeed! I mean this was something she never did!

It took a lot of work and a bit of concern but between the "A" and her reaction, it was well worth it. I left school that day in a really good mood. My dad was equally as happy when I got home and told him all about it. Just because it looks like your down it doesn't mean you're out. Just because something looks impossible doesn't mean it's not still possible.

MR. SNAIL

GOING TO THE PERIOD before last with Mr. Snail was always a mission. I dreaded every second, every minute, and every day of his class. Whenever I raised my hand to answer or ask a question, he looked at me in disgust. *What was his problem?* There was nothing on my face to be disgusted about. I'm a handsome guy if I do say so myself! That's what my mother tells me, anyway. I was also confused about what disgust you could find with me on the first day of school. I shrugged it off and kept raising my hand without care of his aggravation. I had the correct answer. When you know an answer in school when a teacher asks a question, you raise your hand.

Maybe he was disgusted about the fact that I was the only one in his class of 30 who cared and had a clue about history and what he was "teaching." **PSA – GIVING PACKETS OF WORK TO CHILDREN TO SILENTLY COMPLETE IS NOT TEACHING!** I like to call teachers that just give worksheets packet teachers.

I don't know why he continued to give us packet, after packet, after packet, after packet. Half of the class did not do it anyway. The other half of the class minus me did it incorrectly. When it was time to go over the packet of work, you could tell he hated it. He felt this way because no one ever had an answer. No one would raise their hand to answer his question. No one except for me, and it burned him up. I could tell it when he looked at me, when he ignored me, and when he kept talking. Ask me if I cared? Nope I didn't at all! **PSA – IF STUDENTS AREN'T ANSWERING TEACHERS QUESTIONS OR**

**DON'T SEEM TO CARE ABOUT WHAT TEACHERS ARE
TEACHING, THEN PERHAPS TEACHERS SHOULD DO
SOMETHING DIFFERENT!!!**

Fast forward to the end of the year. It was time for our culminating (end of the year) test. Mr. Snail asked us what day we would prefer to have this gigantic test he had to give us. He went on and on about how it was going to have all of the material he taught us all year long on it. He gave us a choice between June 13th and June 17th. Being that my birthday is on the 17th of June I definitely did not want to take a test on my birthday. Who would?

Mr. Snail broadcasted, "As you know we have our final coming up. By a show of hands, who wants the test on the 13th?"

Of course, I raised my hand for the 13th. I was surprised that I was the only one that did so.

Mr. Snail proclaimed a second time, "By a show of hands, who wants the test on the 17th?" This time no one raised a hand. LOL! *No one really wanted to take the test on either day (including me) but since choices were being passed out I wanted the 13th. My class was being funny and I was glad about this. I knew it was going to work to my advantage. I knew exactly what was coming up next.*

Mr. Snail nodded and said, "Since Joshua is the only one who voted, and he wants the test on the 13th that's when we will have it. Everyone moaned and groaned at me. But, I had a huge smile on my face.

I was like, "Thank-you because I don't want to take a test on my birthday".

Angrily Brianna said, "Don't nobody care 'bout yo birthday."

My rebuttal, "A lot of people care about my birthday. And we won't be taking a test on my birthday. And nobody cares about the fact that you have a 0% chance of hair growth so you have to buy weave that you obviously can't afford by the looks of your hair now!" *As soon as it came out of my mouth, I felt awful. I knew it was mean and I shouldn't have said it. My parents taught me way better than this. The only thing I could use to condone my action is that she had been running her mouth all year*

and I was tired of it. Not to mention that she tried to play
me about my birthday.

"OOOOWWWWWW!" the rest of the class screamed. Mr. Snail did not say a word. He just walked across the class shaking his head at both Gyeamma and I. Now I had done it. It took the entire year. Today, at almost the last few weeks of school I had finally given him something to be disgusted about. Guess what? At this point...I REALLY DIDN'T CARE! When you look for something hard and long enough you will find it.

This would be my first and last year here at this school. Oh what a year it was. I didn't learn much academically but I sure had a lot of other lessons. This year was more about life learning than academics. This year was more about sharpening up on come back lines than academics. This year was about me seeing that there is always something or in this case someone around who can bring light to a dark situation. This year was about in the words of my mother "building my character and growing me up in a different way." You see I was angry most of the time at this school and wanted to put many of these teachers in their place. They weren't teaching me anything and they were not nice to children. I wanted to tell them all off just about every day. I wanted to tell them that just because you're teaching in the hood doesn't mean you should be giving us packets. Just because you're teaching in the hood, it doesn't mean you can talk to us like s**t. Just because we go to school in the hood it doesn't mean we are not important! We can change the world too! We are the future! I wanted to ask them why they were even here teaching in my community in the first place if they weren't going to be really teaching. I wanted to tell them you didn't teach me a da** thing all year. I said none of these things. I walked out of this school for the last time knowingly happy that I would only be back to visit. I felt bad for friends and acquaintances that I was leaving behind to face these teachers again next year. I knew things weren't going to change much. The truth is although the year was difficult on many different days; I wouldn't change it for the world.

{ 6 }

OUT OF THE HOOD AND UP THE STREET

YES I HAD LEFT that embarrassment of a school and moved with my mother to a town called Buckley. She had determined that the schools in this town were pretty good and in her words, "conducive to a good free public education". This town was more white then my previous school. We had an expectation.

The school was a few blocks down the street from my house. This was very convenient since I would be going to and from school solo. I really enjoyed this distance from home. This actually was one of the highlights of my 6th grade experience; the walk to and from school. My school was called Johnson Petrone Elementary School.

On the first day, I walked into this new school with a positive and open mindset. *This year was going to be different. I'm going to learn a lot. I am going to get along with my teachers. I am going to stay positive. I have a growth mindset.*

All of this quickly shifted when I walked into homeroom with Mr. Rom. Now I had a different situation to deal with. I was the only Black kid in my class. SMH! *Highlight! Target! All eyes on me!* My classmates were looking me up and down as I entered. *I was the only scoop of chocolate ice -cream in a tub of vanilla. I was the only black spot on the Dalmatian.* No, the looks weren't welcoming at all. They were more like a question. They were more like look at this visitor from another planet. They were like who are you and what are you doing in our school? I later found out that many of these kids had been together since Kindergarten. Essentially, I was an outsider to them.

I didn't care about any of it though, not their opinions, not their questioning looks and not their stares. I kind of liked the attention. I knew as the year went on they would be staring at me differently, in a good way.

"We have a new student I want to introduce to you today class," Mr. Rom announced, "His name is Joshua Stephen! He is from.... He is from....," he repeated.

He was expecting me to answer so I did, "Radishon, I am from Radishon."

"OHHHHH so you are a product of the Radishon Public School System?" he asked in surprise.

"Ummmm, I'm a product of how my family raised me," was my response. The class looked at me wide eyed. I wasn't supposed to say what I said but I did.

Mr. Rom rolled his eyes at me and said, "Okay moving on, let's get to the math."

He gave us a packet and said, "You guys should know this based on your prior knowledge." As soon as he said that I was terrified. *The truth is I didn't learn any math last year. Ms. Slims couldn't teach math and didn't. She yelled do the work all day. She had us chant Nas every time we came in the class, but teach math she did not do.* He handed out the packet and I was mind-blown.

The packet was full of rates, ratios, and algebraic equations. *I barely learned place value at a high level. How was I supposed to do this?* For me getting through this packet work was a DISASTER! I watched all of the other kids in my new class breeze through the whole thing. I was still on problem two. I was frustrated.

It was time for gym so thankfully I got away from the math. I was glad to feel the fresh air hit my face as we left our classroom trailer to go inside of the building for gym. For a moment I felt sadness for all of my friends I left in Radishon. We didn't learn a thing in math last year or any other subject for that matter. I knew they still weren't learning a thing in that school now and especially not any math. I could only hope it was going to be better for them this year, but chances were slim.

My thoughts were quickly interrupted by the girls who would not stop talking about how much they hated their parents or their drama with other kids in the school.

Their conversation would go something like this, "OMG! I hate Janae soooooooo much. She took Brianna's boyfriend but he cheated on her with her younger sister."

"OMG! Bruno is sooooo hot," another would say.

Are you sure I am in the 6ᵗʰ grade? I thought I left the drama free school community. I quickly learned I left one style of drama for another. This was supposed to be better. To a certain extent it was better, but to another it was not.

{ 7 }

MR. ROM, I KNOW I CAN'T TEACH MATH SECOND EDITION

JUDGING BY WHAT WENT down in homeroom with Mr. Rom, clearly he already had an opinion about me. I guess nothing good was supposed to come out of Radishon. I guess he already expected me to be a problem for him and the class because I was from Radishon. I guess I was supposed to be nothing but a dumb Black Boy, who doesn't know nothing because I came from Radishon. But what else is new? I have seen all this before and felt this before. It was the first day of school yet again and I already felt profiled, categorized, summed up and misread.

Plus, I was still struggling over this packet. I knew I was going to get a bad grade on it but I turned it in anyway. It was time for ELA to begin. This was my subject! I could prove myself here. Being that my mom is an ELA teacher and drilled everything ELA in my head, I would have English Language Arts on lock. At least that is what I thought until we got these books that looked as dense as the Bible. I enjoyed reading, but I was already dreading reading this book.

"Read pages 110 – 170 and answer the 20 questions about the text for homework," Mr. Rom commanded. He continued, "If I don't have it by tomorrow morning, it's a big fat ZERO!" A common threat among teachers had been thrown at me again.

I was shocked about this workload with no real teaching to go with it. You already know, I hate when teachers just give students packets of work or a bunch of work sheets to keep us busy, like that's good teaching.

Why was I so surprised? I mean he had already assigned us some math that seemed like it was for high-school students.

The next day at school, morning announcements were made over the loud speaker. When everyone was asked to please stand for the Pledge of Allegiance we all stood up. We all faced the flag and most everyone put their right hand across their heart. I was not included with everyone. What I mean is, I did stand up straight and tall, and I did face the flag. Instead of placing my right hand across my heart, I held my fist in hand behind my back. As we sat down I glanced over at Mr. Rom, whose eyes were already burning a hole in my back. If looks could cut and kill I would be bleeding and dead. I could tell he wasn't liking what I did at all.

"Joshua, get over here!" he said irritably while also directing me to him with his pointer finger. "Why wasn't your hand on your heart during the Pledge?" he questioned.

"It's a prerogative Mr. Rom. If I choose to pledge or not. I wasn't disrespectful in anyway way so there should be no problem," I replied back. *There was so much more I could say and wanted to say about this but I didn't. I just thought. Does this country pledge its allegiance to me and my race? Does it respect black and brown children like me? I am doing well by even showing respect because that comes from home training. I wouldn't be telling the truth if I pledged allegiance. I would be going against my personal belief system, which I am entitled to have if I put my hand over my heart. As a black boy in America the truth is I'm not safe. I'm not safe. No allegiance has been pledged to keep me safe.*

None of this sat well with him but honestly I didn't care. I wasn't drawing attention to myself. I was looking at the flag. My parents taught me to speak up for myself, follow my convictions, and do it respectfully among so many other things. All of this was exactly what I was doing. This is exactly what I would continue doing!

LUNCH AND MR. DJ

I T WAS TIME FOR lunch. I stood in the line like everyone else. *Lunch monitors all seemed to be the same no matter where I was in school. They always seemed so mad at the students. For what though? They picked the job!*

"HOT OR COLD?" the lunch monitor snarled.

"What?" I asked in confusion.

"HOT OR COLD," she repeated firmly and in agitation.

"HOT," I responded.

I was then pointed in the direction of a staircase. *Where was I going? These monitors must not have realized I was new to this school. It was lunchtime, I was in the cafeteria, and they pointed me to a staircase leading to a hallway of classes. Unbelievable!* I walked into the direction I was pointed.

I ended up at a classroom where I sat down at a desk and waited for my name to be called. *This was a lot to be doing for lunch.* A few white kids were already in the room so I knew I was in the right place. I didn't think there was going to be any issues.

"Please get out of this class," another lunch lady said to me calmly.

This is crazy. I was being punked for sure. It's lunchtime for goodness sakes! I am hungry. I am walking all over the place. Now I'm being told to leave? The truth is her tone was calmer then the rest of the monitors so I left the classroom.

I didn't want any issues so I did as I was asked. Everyone in the room left as well. When the monitor turned her head, everyone who walked out with me, decided to run back into the room. I stayed in the hallway trying to avoid any drama. It was a good thing that I did. She began screaming her head off. "I SAID GET OUT OF THE CLASS AND YOU DID NOT LISTEN. GO TO MR. DJ'S OFFICE RIGHT NOW," she yelled.

She pointed at me as she said that. You could see her teeth while she screamed. They were so yellow they looked like she had smoked cigarettes since birth. I had a flashback of Ms. Hot Breath. I was sure this monitors breath smelled like a sewer. *Ugh! It was lunchtime I had to think about something else or I would loose my appetite.*

I didn't do anything wrong but still ended up having to walk to Mr. DJ's office with everyone else. I purposely did not go back in the classroom and still ended up being sent to the principal's office. I was being punked. When I saw him, he ordered me to walk in with his finger. *Is this a thing with them?* As soon as I saw Mr. DJ I thought he looked like our 27th president, William H. Taft. I walked into the office, and almost lost my hearing when he slammed the door behind me.

"Sit down," he yelled. I sat down in this sticky uncomfortable chair. I am sure that no one in their right mind would want to sit there. I was actually surprised that this was furniture in his office. He sat down behind his desk and took a deep breath in and exhaled out. He looked like he was relaxing himself. I on the other hand was not relaxed at all. *I didn't even belong in this office.*

"Why are you in my office," he calmly stated.

"Because she, told me to come in here," I confidently responded. *I know there was attitude in my voice and I didn't care.* After that, the lecture began.

"First of all, she has a name, and it's Mrs. King. Second of all, she said that she had to tell you three times, to get out of the class and you refused. Is this correct? Because if her story is true, then I could suspend you for insubordination."

Whooowwww! I was appalled by the magnitude of a first offence. I was also appalled by this lie that I was being tangled up in. My eyes showed it, the lines in my forehead showed it, and my body showed it I'm sure. I calmly told him the whole story. He listened like he was going to be fair. He listened like he wanted to hear what I had to say. But really it was all fake. He already had his mind made up about what my punishment would be.

"Oh wow," he said with wide eyes. He then called for Mrs. King to come into his office. She entered and comfortably sat down. Once she sat down he asked her to explain her side of the story.

She did exactly that and began talking. The funny thing is, actually it wasn't funny at all, was that her story sounded exactly like the one I just heard from Mr. DJ. *No this lady ain't sitting in her telling this story leaving out the fact that I did follow her directions. WOW!* Judging by the look on Mr. DJ's face, I already knew that he thought that her story had more validity to it than mine did. But, I was fine with that because, I knew the truth. He told her to leave, and out the door she went. He got into my face and to my surprise the aroma of mint filled my nose; clearing out all of the congestion that I had.

He got very close and whispered, "I'm going to check the cameras. If I see that you were in the class, then you will be suspended." *Was he trying to scare me*? If so, he failed because I knew that after she told us to get out of the classroom, that's what I did, and I didn't go back.

"Get out of my office," he yelled.

I sauntered out of his office with no worries or thoughts about suspension. I did go back into the cafeteria thinking this is some crazy stuff right here. This white principal has lost his mind. I wonder does he talk to all of the Black kids like this, and assume the worse of them. If either one of my parents hear about this they would be tight. They would be in this school in the principal's office, sitting in the very same chairs I sat in, calling him about his stuff. I decided to leave them uninformed. It was kind of early in the year to have them in the principal's office putting him in his place. I would be just fine. I could handle this one. Besides I was innocent.

{ 9 }

I'M AN AMBASSADOR NOW

IT WAS RAINING ALL morning so we would have indoor recess today. When it was time for recess, we would all have to go to the auditorium. We sat in silence while doing absolutely nothing. Very productive right? It was recess for goodness sakes. This school was just full of great moves.

After a few minutes of being bored beyond belief I got up and walked towards Mr. Rom.

"Mr. Rom, can we bring work or something with us to the auditorium when we have indoor recess?" I asked. "We are sitting here doing nothing. This is not a good use of our time at all".

Mr. Rom looked at me quizzically and said, "Let's go down to Mr. DJ's office."

As we entered the office together, Mr. DJ asked Mr. Rom in exasperation, "What did he do now?"

I looked at Mr. Rom in confusion and annoyance. Here we go again. *Just because I am one of the few black kids in this school and my white teacher and I are going to the principal's office, doesn't mean I am in trouble. This was an offensive comment and it rubbed me the wrong way.*

Mr. Rom chuckled and said, "He is here to ask you a question Mr. DJ. He is not in trouble." *Why did he chuckle? The assumption DJ made was not funny at all. It was actually very racists and offensive. It confirmed the feelings I got around him. I wanted to put them both in their place and walk out of the office. They were the same. Smh!*

I stood up calmly and stated, "I think that we should be able to bring work to the auditorium on "in days" I feel like it will be quieter and most definitely a more productive use of our time."

Mr. DJ must have agreed because he nodded his head and said, "I will make sure to let the "in-day" lunch monitors know about this.

I nodded and left. My mind went back to being angry at his initial response at seeing me at his office. I quickly let it go though. This whole thing was bigger than them and bigger than me. I was able to use my voice to score a huge win for myself and for others. I would be able to get a head start on homework, which would free me up after school. My classmates could do the same if they wished to. SWOOSH! One for the team!

{ 10 }

ROBBED

THE YEAR MOVED RATHER quickly filled with tests and packet teachers. Graduation season had finally arrived and I was happy about it. I was over this year and ready for it to end.

The class received orders to write an essay about their time and experience over the year(s) in elementary school. We had to include feelings about how sad we would be to leave, but how excited we would be to go to middle school. The top three essays writers would be able to participate in the graduation ceremony. The best essay of the three would represent Mr. Rom's class and read their essay in front of the whole graduation crowd. This included all five sixth grade classes, their parents, guardians and other invited guests. The auditorium would be packed. The two other winners would read the names of students in our 6th grade class.

Essays are my thing! I was feeling confident that I was going to be one of the top three essay winners. I was going to have one of the three roles in my graduation ceremony for sure. Within seconds after Mr. Rom finished explaining what we had to do, I began writing. I wrote for the whole weekend and had a bomb essay.

When I think of Johnson Petrone Elementary School a flood of different thoughts and memories come to mind. I'm sure some are thinking he just got here this school year. Others are saying he hasn't been here since Kindergarten like me. Others are saying I know way more teachers than he does. Or they are saying, I have way more memories than him. While all of this may be true, none of this takes away from the impact Johnson Petrone School has had on me, and the place it will always have in my life.

Who could ever forget Mr. Rom? He was my homeroom teacher who taught us every subject in the book. Yes Mr. Rom, the rest of my classmates and I will never forget that, "ORDER MATTERS in division and subtraction". I will always remember the freedom to make mistakes that Mrs. M always gave us in physical education. If anyone could teach someone to love playing sports it would most definitely be Mrs. M. Notes, beats, and measures came alive in music class with Mrs. P. I will always respect her endless talent and her musical abilities. So very impressive!

Making the pinch pots was so much fun in art and will always be a lasting memory thanks to Ms. C. Caring, considerate and has an eye for the children here at Petrone School. This is how I describe my favorite teacher Ms. B. Library was always a time for relaxation and peace thanks to Ms. B. And last but certainly not least our Johnson Petrone School principal Mr. DJ will never ever be forgotten. He always had his eye on me and kept me on my toes. As a result I was always on my best behavior, well most of the time anyway. To all of the other teachers that aren't mentioned because I never met you, thanks for your service to Johnson Petrone School.

My experience at Petrone wouldn't have had the impact that it did on me without my friends. We joked together; we stood outside in the rain together, chilled in the chilly weather, and even went out to lunch together. All of you know who you are! You will never be forgotten.

*As I close I want to say to all of my elementary school classmates... our elementary years are finally over... which is a cause for celebration!!! Let's ride this momentum into the next chapter of our academic lives, which will be a success! I am more than proud to say Middle School ready or not... **HERE WE COME**!!!!!!!!*

I read it to the class and got applauded like I was Kendrick Lamar after performing "HUMBLE." Everyone had a chance to share their essay to the class. After we all read them Mr. Rom told us that everyone had a good essay. He made a point to tell us that only three of them were great.

"I will only be selecting great essays," he proclaimed. The person who will be reading their essay at graduation is... drum roll please... Teth!"

Yes I was disappointed. Everyone knew that I had the best essay by far. Of course my teacher didn't see it that way because he selected Teth, his favorite.

"The other two that will be announcing the names are, Dayla and Joshua," he announced.

I had been cheated but I was still happy that I got picked for something. Like I said I had the best essay and everyone knew it. I had my classmates in tears for goodness sakes. In the back of my head stuck my reality. I was the new Black kid in a mostly white school. My chances were slim to none of being picked to begin with and I knew it. It was all good though. I know I say this a lot but I have to. It keeps me settled most of the time. There would be other opportunities for me to display my writing gift in front of people.

Later on when it was time to go to lunch, Mr. Rom pulled me aside and whispered, "Listen, I'm going out on a limb by letting you do this you know. You have been in the principals' office too many times this year. Many people including Mr. DJ have told me not to let you do this. But I am going to let you do this anyway. Make sure you do the job and do it well."

Really? Did he just say this to me? Some of those times, it wasn't even my fault. Some of those times I wasn't even in trouble. I smiled and told him okay thank you and made sure that everything I did from that point on was the perfect and the right move to make. The way they operated around here, the way they had eyes on me, one little slip up would have had me out of the graduation ceremony in a heartbeat.

IT'S TIME TO SAY GOODBYE

FTER A WEEK OF prepping and practicing for graduation, it was finally time for the real deal. The whole five-class grade of us sang God Bless America. Immediately after Dayla and I got up and walked to the podium. It was time for us to announce the names of our classmates. We sorted out between the two of us who was going to read what. Dayla wanted to read the top half of names, which was fine with me. That left me reading the bottom half.

Dayla stepped up to the podium and began. "It is with great honor and pride that we introduce Mr. Rom's class graduates. Rihanna Catalina, Teth Christmas, David Christmas, Riles Granellis, Jarl Cillarin, Calamari Lewis, Romeo Mandsdillo, and I am Dayla Roberts." No one clapped. Everyone was supposed to save the applause until the end.

When she was finished I stepped up onto the podium. "Tathew Nocherino, Wack Tucker, Verona Touseff, Jeric Jesus, Taydon Javion, Costanlina Jemima, Victorious Biggie, and I am Joshua Stephens. The audience went wild like we just performed Rockstar by Post Malone.

We sang the rest of our songs and finished up the rest of our program. There were a bunch of snacks and waters outside for us after the ceremony. We took pictures with each other, smiled, laughed, and enjoyed the moment.

There were a lot of up hill battles to overcome. I still wouldn't trade the experience for anything. I knew I was being prepared for something great and all of these events were important pieces of my life puzzle. I came from Ms. Hot Breath to Mr. Rom in a matter of two years. All I can say is I'm glad I made it out and I graduated. I finally finished elementary school and everything it had to offer. I was heading to a new building; beginning a new chapter, ready to start a new year! Because of that, I'm hittin' the shoot, I'm milly rocking, and I'm dabbing.

ABOUT THE AUTHOR

NTELLECTUAL, DYNAMIC, ATHLETIC, AND compassionate are just a few words to describe this young Haitian American versatile author. This is Darrell's first large scale published work, however, he is not new to writing.

His literacy foundation began at an early age when he first discovered his love for listening to and reading books. Even then he understood and appreciated what a good book has to offer its reader. By the age of twelve Etienne had already attended six different schools, some in the inner city and some in the suburbs, which allowed him to develop a unique perspective on schooling and teachers. He was easily able to transfer these experiences into his writing. Excelling in school based English Language Arts (ELA) instruction is second nature to Darrell. This is reflected most vividly in his academic record, which consistently boasts of mastery and excellence. At the tender age of nine Darrell participated in a school wide Paw Printer writing project. In this he wrote a story of his experience with his then soccer coach and accompanied it with illustrations. It was clear then that a budding writer was in the making. A hot bed of talent and creativity Darrell Nicolas Etienne Jr. not only writes books but he is an up and coming songwriter as well. Stay tuned for more to come from this potential laden phenomenon.

Printed in the United States
By Bookmasters